Wake up and open your eyes

PHOENIX YOUNG READERS LIBRARY

1.	The Sun and the Wind	Anne Matindi
2.	Cock and Lion	Kalondu Kyendo
3.	The Peacock and the Snake	Elijah K. Soi
4.	The Valley of the Dead	Akberali Manji
5.	The Battle of Mogori	Zaccheaus arap Kimeto
6.	The Greedy Host	J.K Njoroge
7.	Tales of Wamugmno	P.N. Kuguru
8.	Mzee Nyachote	Roeland Japuonjo
9.	The Proud Ostrich	J K. Njoroge
10.	The Fly Whisk	Stephen Gichuru
11.	The Orange Thieves	Chanty Dahal
12.	The Magic Stone	J. Ibongia & L. Dobrin
13.	Beautiful Nyakio	Fredrick Ndung'o
14.	The Speck of Gold	Cynthia Hunter
15.	The Children of the Forest	Joel Makumi
16.	The Girl Who Couldn't Keep a Secret	Clare Omanga
17.	The Powerful Magician	Daniel Irungu
18.	Give the Devil his Due	W.K. Boruett
19.	The Talking Devil	Leo Odera Omoio
20.	Njogu the Prophet	Jamlick Mutua
21.	The Adventures of Thiga	C M. Mureith'
22.	The Coconut Girl	Joseph Kabui
23.	Wake Up and Open Your Eyes	Edwara Muhire
24.	The River Without Frogs	Writers' Committee
25.	Lots of Wonders	Sam Mbure
26.	Anna the Air Hostess	Cynthia Hunter
27.	Captured by Raiders	Benjamin S. Wegesa
28.	The Town Tricksters	David Mwaurah
29.	Tit for Tat	J.K. Njoroge
30.	Njaga the Town Monkey	Joel Makumi
31.	The Girl who Became Chief	A.O. Isoka
32.	The Vanishing Potatoes	Cynthia Hunter
33.	The Kasiwes and their Animals	Anne Matindi
34.	Jimmy the Jeep	Betty Mwanza
35.	End of the Beginning	Joel Makumi
36.	The Cruel Burden	Okoth Gonza

and more.............many more

Wake up and open your eyes

Edward Muhire

Illustrations: Chris Ochieng

Cover: Julius Maina

PHOENIX PUBLISHERS, NAIROBI

First published in 1976
First Phoenix edition published in 1989 by
Phoenix Publishers Ltd.,
Mellow Heights, Ngara Road,
P.O. Box 30474-00100,
Nairobi, Kenya.

ISBN 9966 47 080 8

Reprinted in 1990, 1991, 1993, 1994, 1996, 1998, 1999, 2000, 2002, 2003, 2007, 2010, 2011, 2012, 2014, 2016, 2018

Printed by:
Ramco Printing Works Ltd
P.O Box 27750 - 00506
Nairobi, Kenya

Contents

Chapter 1

Higiro's Early Days

In the village of Baale, Rwanda, in 1945, a boy called Higiro was born. His mother died at his birth, so he was brought up by his grandmother. His father completely neglected the boy and very soon married a young girl, Frola Gakunga. This young girl was to be Higiro's step-mother, but she could not give him the mother's love that he needed.

When Frola Gakunga was first married, she used to go and see Higiro at his grandmother's small hut, but as soon as she gave birth to her first child, she stopped paying these visits, and Higiro had no one to care for him except his old grandmother.

Many people in the village said that the boy would die, but although his grandmother was old, she looked after him well. When he was five years old, he was big enough and strong enough to help her fetch water and dig in the garden. It was then that Higiro's father and step-mother started to show an interest in him, and his father went to visit the grandmother's house.

The old woman did not feel very happy about his visit, but she said politely, "Come in and sit by the fire. It's cold outside."

"I shan't stay long," said Higiro's father. "I'll just sit down and tell you why I've come."

Higiro was playing outside and when he heard a strange man's voice in their hut. He ran in to find out who was talking to his grandmother.

"Who is this man, mother?" he asked, gripping her arm in fear.

"Go to the well and fetch me some water," the grandmother replied. "I'll tell you who it is before you go to bed."

Higiro took his small water pot and ran to the well.

"He doesn't even know who I am!" exclaimed his father when he was out of hearing.

"That's not his fault. You never visit us, that's why he doesn't know you," said grandmother. "Now what did you come to tell me?"

"I came about the boy. I want to have my son back," said Higiro's father.

"I shan't let him go," replied the old woman firmly. "He'll stay with me until he's old enough to look after himself."

"I know the child means everything to you and he helps you a great deal with your work," said Higiro's father. "I also know I didn't look after him when he was very young, nevertheless, a child belongs to his father. Higiro belongs to me and my clan."

When the grandmother heard these words, she grew hot with rage. "Leave my poor hut and return to your big house," she said. "Tomorrow we'll go to the chief of the village. He'll listen to what I have to say."

Higiro's father was disappointed by his mother's attitude, but he went away without any more arguments. Grandmother was grieved by his visit. She was old but full of courage and was determined not to part with Higiro. She had nursed him when he was a baby and given him the love he needed. Now he was useful to her and she would not let him go. She did not sleep well that night as she could not stop thinking of Higiro's father's visit. Early the next morning, she went to the chief and told him the whole story. When she had finished, she wept in front of him.

"Don't cry, old woman," said the chief. "I'll settle your trouble tomorrow. Go home and buy a pot of beer and I'll call together the elders of the village and we'll talk to Higiro's father."

The following day, the elders, Higiro's father and step-mother and grandmother met the chief outside his house.

"Listen to me," began the old grandmother.

"Old woman, I shall speak to my visitors first, and you will speak when I ask you," the chief interrupted her.

"My friends," he began. "This old woman has a problem which she wants us to help her to settle. Let's hear her speak."

"Yes, yes, let's hear her speak," agreed everyone present.

The old woman then stood up. "My friends, you all know I've looked after this boy, Higiro, since he was a tiny baby. His mother died when he was born and his father gave him to me to look after. He neither came to see him nor helped him in any way, so Higiro grew up without knowing his father's love. Now he's grown into a fine young lad and can help me with the work on the shamba but his father wants to take him away. He came for him yesterday and I refused to let the boy go. I want to keep this child until he's old enough to look after himself. I want to hear what you have to say. What is your advice?"

There was a long silence. Then one of the old men spoke. "The old woman is right in what she says, but our customs are such that a child belongs to a man, not to a woman. Higiro's father should buy a white cow, two black goats, a cock and a hen and give them to the grandmother. Then the boy should go back to his father."

"You have spoken well," said the chief. "Do you agree to that, old woman?"

She looked at Higiro and Higiro looked at her.

"You say a child belongs to a man," said the grandmother. "But will his father look after him properly? If you all think so, I'll let him go."

"He'll have everything he needs," said Higiro's father. Everyone laughed loudly at this. Then they were silent again until the chief spoke.

"This is then settled my friends," he said. "The old woman will be given a white cow, two black goats, a cock and a hen and then Higiro will go to his father. Does everybody agree?"

"Yes, yes," they all said, and nodded their heads. Then the beer was passed round again before they went back to their homes.

"Grandmother, where do you want to take me?" asked Higiro.

"I want you to stay, but your father wants you to go to his home," she said.

"Who is my father? The tall man with a beard?"

"Yes, that's him and his name is Bucumi."

"I don't want to go and live with him," said Higiro. "I won't go!"

"Yes, child, you must go," said grandmother. "He'll kill me if you don't go."

"But you'll be all alone in the hut," said Higiro.

"I'll keep the two goats with me, so I'll be all right," said the grandmother.

But that night Higiro could not sleep for fear of leaving his grandmother alone in the small hut. He kept thinking of a dream he had had, of a wild animal running away with one of the goats.

A week after the meeting with the chief, Bucumi and two of his friends brought the cow, goats and cock and hen to the old woman. When Higiro knew his father had come for him, he asked his grandmother if he could go to the well and get her some water.

"No child, you need a rest before you leave here," said the old woman. Then she turned to Bucumi and said, "Take the boy and send him to school. I don't know how to read or write but he should learn. He's in your care now. If anything happens to him it's nothing to do with me. Higiro!" she called. "Your father wants to go now."

As soon as Higiro heard this, he ran out of the house into the bush and hid where they could not find him. They searched until dark and then decided they would have to leave him until the next day.

"Don't worry," said the grandmother. "He'll come back tonight and I'll bring him to your house tomorrow."

When Bucumi left, Higiro came out of his hiding-place.

"Grandmother, I won't go to that man's house, I don't like him," he said.

"Come and have your food, child," said the old woman smiling. "I knew where you were all the time, but I didn't tell him."

Higiro felt happy again, so he had his supper and went to bed.

The following evening, the old woman told him to get ready to go and visit a friend of hers. She tied up Higiro's belongings in a bundle and they set off, but Higiro did not know they were going to his father's house until they arrived and were greeted by his step-mother.

The village people clapped their hands and cried, "The lost one is back home again."

An old woman caught hold of Higiro and lifted him up and down while the rest of the villagers sang traditional songs to show how happy they were to see the boy back with his father.

"My friends, I have brought the child to his home," said the old woman. "I have done my part and cared for him well. It is now up to his father to look after him."

Then she prepared to leave, but Higiro started to follow her. "You want to leave me here?" asked the boy.

"You must stay with your parents, my grandson," she said. "But I'll come back and see you tomorrow. God stay with you."

His step-mother gripped his arm as the old woman made her way home. Higiro struggled to escape but his step-mother held onto him and locked him in one of the rooms. Higiro beat on the walls, the door, the floor and then cried until he fell asleep. Grandmother did not come to visit Higiro the next day and after a while he became used to his new home.

Chapter 2

School Days

One of the reasons why Bucumi wanted to have his son with him was because he thought he should go to school. Higiro was very pleased, partly because he disliked his step-mother and her children and did not want to stay at home with them all day. His father bought him a new uniform and told him he must keep it clean and not let the other children pull it and tear it.

The night before he was to start school, Higiro went to bed early and thought of himself in his new uniform playing with the other children. He woke up early in the morning, washed and dressed before his father had woken up.

Bucumi took Higiro to school, talked to the Headmaster and paid the fees.

"Now, you stay here all day," Bucumi said to his son. "You can walk home with Gisitu and Hamisi. They're in your class and they don't live far from us."

His father then left him and for the first time Higiro
was afraid. He looked round at the buildings, the boys
and the teachers, but he wouldn't talk to anybody. He
stayed by himself all day. A bell rang and the children
were told to go to their classrooms. Higiro followed

the two boys Gisitu and Hamisi, and sat at his desk eager to see his teacher.

A tall, slim, young woman walked into the classroom and said, "Good morning. My name is Miss Kabeera. Now I want to learn you names. I'll start with the front row."

She wrote down all the names as the children called them out. Then lessons began and Higiro listened intently to Miss Kabeera. He was keen to learn all he could. At the end of the day, all the new pupils were told to go into the hall and the Headmaster spoke to them.

"Good afternoon children," said the Headmaster. "I welcome you to this school and I want you to know that every day you must be here by 8 o'clock. Anyone who comes late will be reported to me and will be beaten. Some days you will be given a special task. Tomorrow you will each bring five reeds. Now remember, don't be late."

The Headmaster then dismissed the children and Higiro ran home by himself. When he got home, he found his step-mother playing with her children.

"Where is my food?" he asked.

"There's no food here for you," she replied. "Don't ask me for food again. I'm not your servant."

Higiro was so hungry, he burst out crying. There was nobody to comfort him and he was very miserable indeed.

"Take the water pot to the well if you want to eat," she said. "Then you can wait for your food at supper time. If you don't fetch enough water, you won't have any food."

Higiro was so tired and so hungry that he cried even more and he could not control himself. Then he thought he must find his father at once. He ran to the banana plantation but he was not there. He ran to the potato garden but he was not there either. Where was he? Then Higiro remembered that he often went hunting in the afternoons, and he probably was still in the forest. He ran back to the cassava field and dug out a root and ate it uncooked. He felt better as he walked back to the house and was pleased to find his father had returned.

Supper was going to be delicious. Bucumi had killed an antelope and told his wife they would all have a big share.

At supper time, Higiro's step-mother said, "My husband, your son is very greedy. Look at the way he eats. He looks as if he's had nothing since early morning."

"Father, we hardly had anything at school," Higiro said. "I only had half a cup of porridge for my lunch and my step-mother refused to give me anything when I came home. I looked everywhere for you but I could not find you."

His step-mother was furious. She pulled Higiro away from the table and tried to push him out of the room.

"How dare you say you found no food at home," she said.

"Leave the boy alone and let him finish his supper," Bucumi said firmly. "Then he can go to bed."

Higiro sat down again, but now he did not feel hungry and ate slowly. His step-mother grumbled at him again. "You see, he doesn't really want the food. Look at him picking at it, bit by bit!"

And when Higiro did get up, she gave him a painful smack as he went out of the room.

"Husband, that child is a bad boy. I don't like him

and he doesn't like me. The best thing to do would be to send him back to his grandmother."

"We'll think it over, wife," replied Bucumi. "I'm very tired and I'm going to bed now. Leave me alone."

The days went on, turning into weeks and months, and Higiro stayed with his father and step-mother and continued to go to school. He only made one friend at school — a boy called Gimiyu. He liked him because Gimiyu brought food to school for him. Gimiyu liked Higiro because he helped him with his school work, as Higiro was clever and did all his work quickly. He was particularly good at reading and writing and he was also the best in the class at story-telling.

The last day of term arrived and the Headmaster spoke to the children at the final assembly.

"Today we close school so you can go home for the holidays and have a break from lessons. When you first arrived here, your heads were empty, but now we have filled them with knowledge." Both the children and the teachers laughed at this.

"I hope you will all have a good holiday and come back in good health. Before you go, there are three boys I want to see in my office." He read out the names and made it clear it was because their fees had not been paid.

"Finally I shall read out the names of the children who have done exceptionally well this term."

He opened the report forms and read out three names. The first one was Higiro. "Come here, boy," he said.

Higiro walked up to the platform and shook hands with the Headmaster.

"Here's your report," said the Headmaster. "You should be proud of it, and see that you keep up this standard."

Then he handed him a mug and a packet of biscuits.

"These are for you too. Take everything home to show your parents."

When the other two pupils had received their reports and presents, the children clapped heartily. Higiro was proud and happy and ran home as fast as he could. He went by himself because he did not want anyone to eat his biscuits. He wanted to open the packet in front of his father and share them with him. But, of course, his step-mother saw him first.

"Husband, I told you that this boy would bring trouble to us," she said. "Come and see what he's stolen from the shops on his way home."

"Father, I didn't steal anything! The Headmaster gave me this mug and the packet of biscuits."

"How could that be possible? You're not the only child in the school," said his step-mother.

"Presents were given to the three best ones," he said.

Father read through the report. "You've done well," he said.

"Done well—at school?" shouted Higiro's step-mother. "I'll teach you to do well in the kitchen."

Bucumi, however, was delighted and embraced his son and praised him, and went back to make peace with his quarrelsome wife.

Higiro never went back to that school as the family had to move from Rwanda to Uganda. His father could not put up with the conditions at home any longer, and he had been to Uganda before and knew it was a peaceful country. His father agreed to go with some other families, their plans were made quickly and in a few days they started their journey.

Chapter 3

The Journey to Uganda

It was the middle of the night when the families started off. The whole neighbourhood was asleep, and no one knew of their plans. Thirty people altogether walked quietly out of the village to their unknown destination. They travelled through the night until the light brought the following morning. The children were crying for food and the mothers were tired and hungry. Higiro had grown weak and could walk no more.

"Father, I'm so thirsty! Can I have some water?" he asked.

"We'll go and ask the people in this village if they will give us some," he said.

It was the village of Buhindiri and the people were rather suspicious of the travellers. However, they gave them some water and took no further notice of them. They drank the water and ate the food they had brought with them.

After some hours, they stopped again to rest, and Higiro's father said they had another ten miles to go before they reached the place where they could hire a lorry to take them to Uganda.

"Everyone must have his 35 shillings ready for the journey for his family and all their luggage," he said. "Then when we reach Buganda, we'll go and see a man I used to **work** for. He's Waliggo and lives in Bugerere county. That's where we'll settle."

"How shall we get work there?" one of the men asked.

"This rich man will employ us all," said Higiro's father. "He owns a big shamba with sugar-cane, coffee trees and cotton. He'll have plenty of work for all of us, and the children as well."

Everyone started to get excited and talked about the man who was to employ them all. How rich he must be and what a big shamba he must have.

Higiro began to feel desperately tired and his legs ached badly.

"Father," he called. "I don't think I can walk any farther. My legs hurt so much."

"I can't carry you," replied his father. "I've too much luggage. Come on now, behave like a man. We'll stop for another rest soon."

His step-mother, who had left him alone up to now, heard him and asked sarcastically, "How is it that no one's tired except you, you rascal?"

"Don't upset him at this time," said his father.

"He thinks he's such an important member of the

family. He behaves as if he's the only son you have. I can't do anything with him," said his step-mother.

No one answered and they walked on in silence. Higiro tried to push his aching legs forward without making any more fuss. Everyone was tired and they all walked in silence, the weaker groups gradually falling behind.

"We'll stop here and rest," said Bucumi as darkness was falling. "But we mustn't sleep here as there are so many robbers in this place. It's near the border, so they can easily get away. Two of us will go and fetch the lorry that will take us over to Buganda."

Before long, the lorry arrived and everybody stood up with excitement. For many people, it was their first ride in a moving vehicle.

"I'll take you to the place in Buganda where you want to go," said the driver. "As long as you pay me enough money," he added. Only Bucumi understood his language and asked him how much he would charge to take them to Bugerere.

"We want to go to the rich man, Waliggo," said Bucumi. "You must know where he lives. He has such a large shamba. Everybody knows him."

"Yes, yes!" said the lorry driver. "I know him. I'll charge you five hundred shillings for the journey. Remember, I've got to come back again. Now get in quickly. There are many thieves in this area, and they'll rob you of your money and all your belongings if you stay here. Let the women climb in first."

Bucumi turned to his fellow-travellers and interpreted what the driver had said. This made them all very frightened, as it was now nearly dark. They threw in their bags and parcels and baskets and then the women scrambled up the steps, followed quickly by the men.

The driver was a cunning man, as he instilled fear in them by the mention of robbers so that they would hurry up and get in the lorry without arguing about the price. The driver started the engine and drove at a terrific speed as it grew darker and darker and colder and colder. They passed through very lonely forest country, where nothing lived except birds and monkeys. Mosquitoes flocked inside the lorry in dozens and annoyed the passengers with their constant biting.

Higiro and all the other children soon fell asleep, and so did the women and girls. The fathers went on singing and laughing for a long time, until they too, were rocked to sleep by the rhythm of the engine.

The driver stopped the lorry and the sleepers awoke. They thought something had gone wrong with the lorry, or they had run out of petrol. But nothing had gone wrong with the lorry. The driver had stopped in the middle of the forest to demand more money. He went up to Bucumi and asked for double the amount.

"I want one thousand shillings, tell your people. And they can pay me now or they can get out and I'll leave them to be eaten by the animals of the forest."

Then the driver said that he would not accept payment until they had all climbed out of the lorry. Then they were all scared that they would be left in the forest in the dark, so every man and woman fumbled in their clothes and pockets until Bucumi had collected the thousand shillings. When he had given this to the driver, they were all allowed to get onto the lorry again and the driver grinned happily and started off once more.

The people were helpless but very angry.

"He's a robber," said one.

"He's a rogue," said another.

"I hope all the people we meet away from our home village aren't going to be like that," cried yet another.

"We've been swindled!" they said.

They travelled on in silence as there was nothing they could do, but they kept on grumbling, even as dawn was approaching.

"We worked hard for that money," said a young girl.

"Yes that's true, but we can work for some more as long as there's life in us," answered an older man.

The sun rose, it became hotter and the children cried for water, but no one dared to ask the driver to stop, in case he played his mean trick again and demanded yet more money before he went on. Luckily for the passengers, the driver himself felt thirsty and also wanted a smoke. He stopped the lorry in a village by some small shops and told everyone to get out and buy what they wanted. They all tumbled down, chatting and laughing and found a small hotel where they could buy something to eat and drink.

"There's the school where the rich man's children go!" shouted Bucumi. "I know this village. I used to buy things for my master in these shops."

They climbed back onto the lorry and after a few more miles they reached the rich man's house. They hoped to see their prospective employer at once, but the house was locked, as everybody was working in the fields.

"What shall we do now, Bucumi?" asked his wife.

"The master will be working hard," replied Bucumi. "This is the season of coffee picking, and coffee-growers work from first light till dark. We had better wait until he returns from the fields."

Everybody sat down in the shade of some trees near the house, and the children played around, glad to be free after their long journey. At sunset the master came back with his workers. They were all carrying baskets full of coffee beans.

"That's him," said Bucumi indicating a short man, wearing a dirty kanzu. "That's Mr. Waliggo."

But Mr. Waliggo did not recognize Bucumi at first, and wondered who all these strange people were. His wife came along and she remembered Bucumi.

"This is the boy who used to take our goats to graze. He's a man now, and look, he's grown a beard!"

Then Mr. Waliggo remembered Bucumi, and they all started talking at once.

"Yes, I can give work to you and all your friends," he said. "I'll find you somewhere to live until you're able to build huts for your families."

He was very kind and gave them food and water and then they all knelt down together and thanked God for bringing them safely to the end of their journey.

Chapter 4

Tragedy Strikes

There was plenty of work for all the people on the rich man's shamba, and the following morning they were chosen for different jobs, some to pick coffee, some to dig vegetables, some to pick bananas. Higiro was told he could either go with his father and help him dig, or stay with his step-mother and look after the children. The women had to go to work and then rush back and cook a meal for their husbands.

How did these people manage to communicate with the local people? At first it was difficult and they had to use signs. Then they learnt a few words of Luganda, and every day they learnt more words and could speak better.

After three months, the village was stricken by drought. Food became scarce and there was no water. It was no good working for food, because there was none to be had. Disease broke out and many people died. Bucumi asked the land-owner if he had any medicine against this sickness, but the man said that nothing could be done and the disease always attacked strangers.

"It is not only disease, but we're hungry as well," said Bucumi. "We'll do extra work if you can give us food."

"That's impossible," said the man. "We've hardly enough food for our own family. Tell the people to try somewhere else for food."

Bucumi turned sadly away and when he reached his hut, he lay down. All day he had had a bad pain, and now it had become much worse. He got up in the middle of the night and tried to make a fire, but he was not able to light it. He called his wife.

"Woman, wake up, can't you hear me? Give me some water to drink and make me a fire."

There was no reply from his snoring wife.

"Woman, I'm dying! Wake up, can't you hear me?"

His wife half woke up, but did not hear properly, as she put her head under the blanket to keep out the noise.

"Oh, the pain," cried Bucumi. "Oh the pain!"

This time his voice was so loud that he woke Higiro.

"What's the matter, Father?" he asked.

"Wake your mother up. I'm dying. I must speak to her at once."

Higiro wondered if he could dare wake up his step-mother at this time of night. He knew he would only get a slap for his efforts. Still, he had to risk it, as his father called so urgently.

"Mother, wake up," he cried, standing near her bed. "Father is dying."

Higiro's step-mother woke up in confusion, heard the words and saw Higiro and shouted, "Husband, wake up! Our son Higiro is dying."

"Wife, I've been calling you many times," said Bucumi weakly. "It's not the boy who's dying. It's me! Now wake up and listen to me. Listen to my last words."

Then he coughed as if he was using his last breath.

"Look after Higiro," he said. "I told my master ... I know he's not your own child ... but look after him well. The boy is not of your blood, but if you mistreat him, my spirit will be watching you.—Oh, water! water!"

The woman struggled up and held a cup to Bucumi's lips.

"Higiro, my boy. This is your mother. Stay with her. Now woman, go to my master and tell him I'm dying."

His wife was scared and ran to the big house. It took her a long time to wake up anyone as they were all sleeping soundly. At last Mr. Waliggo came and followed her to her hut.

"There is no life left in him, woman," he said as he bent over Bucumi's body. Everybody was now awake and when they heard the rich man's words, the women and children cried and the men bowed their heads in their hands. Higiro and his step-mother looked alone and lost.

"Bring a blanket to put round the body," ordered Mr. Waliggo. "Tomorrow we shall find some good bark-cloth to bury him in."

The grave was dug the following morning and the dead body was wrapped in bark-cloth and lowered gently into it. The priest was called and he said prayers before the final burial took place. It was then that Higiro knew that he would never see his father again. He did not know where to go and he knew he could not stay happily with his step-mother.

After four days, Waliggo told Higiro that he was going to take him to his brother. "My brother's called

Luutu," he said. "He lives eighty miles from here, and the bus takes us nearly to the door."

Higiro had never travelled on a bus before and he really enjoyed it and was interested in listening to the other passengers talking about politics and all sorts of worldly things. They travelled throughout the day and reached Luutu's house just as he was returning from his work on the shamba.

"Come in and share my tea," he greeted them.

After tea, Waliggo told Higiro to go outside whilst he and his brother discussed their problems.

"You remember me talking about this man, Bucumi, who came from Rwanda with a group of people to work for me?" asked Waliggo. "Well, he died a few days ago, and this is his son. I have brought him to you to look after. Treat him as your son and when he grows up, he will be a great help to you."

"But you've said he had a step-mother. Can't he stay with her?"

"You know how step-mothers behave," went on Waliggo. "Let's help this boy. After all, he's an orphan."

"I know I've no children of my own. But are these people reliable?" asked Luutu. "You remember Wwanye? Well, he adopted an orphan from the same tribe, and when he grew up he ran away with the master's daughter, after stealing two thousand shillings!"

"There's good and bad amongst every people," said Waliggo. "Let's try to help this boy and bring out the good in him. We'll discover his interests and I'm sure we'll succeed."

"Very well, I'll risk it, brother," replied Mr. Luutu. "But if he becomes a nuisance and I find it impossible to bring him up properly, I'll send him back to you."

"He should be good and do what you say. He's young enough to get used to your ways," said his brother.

When they had agreed, Higiro was called in.

"I'm going to leave you with this man," said Mr. Waliggo. "Work hard for him and listen to everything he tells you. If you're obedient and helpful, you'll be able to stay. If you prove to be a nuisance, he'll turn you out to wander in the world alone."

Higiro was sorry to see Waliggo go away and was scared of being left in a strange house. However, he was pleased to be living a long way away from his step-mother, as he knew there would always be trouble between them.

Chapter 5

The Girlfriend

Mr. Luutu loved Higiro as if he were his own son and Higiro came to love him as a father. He converted Higiro to the Catholic belief, so that they could go to church together. He was not a very rich man, but had a small banana plantations coffee shamba and twelve goats.

When he turned twelve years old, Higiro was told to look after these goats. He was warned not to take them into the forest by himself.

"You'll be with other children," said Mr. Luutu. Kato and Maria, our neighbour's children, will go with you. But they were older than him and Higiro was afraid they might fight and abuse him. Then he heard that Kato had run away to work in the Kilembe mines and Higiro thought of escaping too, as he did not want to go into the forest alone with Maria. He planned to run away as soon as he was old enough, but first he decided to go into the forest to graze the goats so he could find out from Maria the way to the mines.

On the first day, Maria came for him and their two herds of goats mingled together. "Share your food with Higiro today," called Mr. Luutu.

"He can bring his own food with him," said Maria.

"He'll bring plenty for you tomorrow," said Mr. Luutu. "Just today, you can share yours."

"Let's go," said Maria, and pushed Higiro forward.

"And don't play about and let the goats wander into people's gardens," said Mr. Luutu. "That's what you did last time with Kato."

The children drove the goats along a small path which led through different shambas. Then they came to a small, green clearing but the girl continued to drive them along.

Higiro was tired of walking. "Can't we stop and let them graze here?" he asked.

"It's too near people's gardens," answered Maria.

"We can look after them," said Higiro.

"We might both fall asleep," said Maria. "Then do you know what will happen? Our parents will be fined, and as for you and me, we'll be beaten to death."

She shuddered and Higiro felt she was really frightened.

"Last time I was tied to a mango tree and beaten," she said, "Because I went to sleep and the goats wandered into people's gardens and ate their crops. We must take them far, far away from here."

Higiro listened with interest. He liked the way she spoke to him and smiled and explained anything he did not understand. They walked on until they came to a place where there was no sign of human settlement. It was a clearing covered with green grass and dotted with trees. The only inhabitants were birds of many colours and sizes.

"Here we are," said Maria. "We can let the goats graze now. Let's sit and watch them."

"We're a long way from home," Higiro remarked. "Let's have our food." He was feeling hungry, but it was not the time that Maria usually had her lunch. "It's too early," she said.

Higiro was tired and hungry and he said so.

"You can eat your share now, if you want to," said Maria. "But I don't have mine till late in the afternoon. That's the time I'm used to having it."

"But we were told to eat together," Higiro reminded her.

"Then you'll have to wait until I feel like eating," she said. Suddenly a monkey appeared. It was a kind that Higiro had never seen before.

"Whatever's that creature?" he asked.

"It's a kind of monkey," replied Maria. "There are a lot of them around here. They like showing off and jumping up and down and hiding so you go and look for them."

"They look like very funny animals. What do they eat?" asked Higiro.

"They eat nearly everything that we eat, but they don't like meat," said Maria. "They steal, fruit and potatoes from people's gardens. They also go into the forest and find nuts and fruit."

It became hotter and hotter and soon it was lunch time. Just as they were going to eat, Higiro pointed to a snake that was wrapped around a tree. Maria gave a small scream and pulled Higiro's arm. "I'm very much afraid of snakes," she said. "They can be dangerous. My brother, Kato, would kill any he saw, but we're too young to do that. If we hit it, it might strike at us."

They took each other's hands and ran away from the snake.

"When did your brother go to the mines at Kilembe?" Higiro asked, when they had gone a safe distance.

"He went long ago," Maria said. "But who told you where he went?"

"My master, Mr. Luutu, told me. If I'd been free, I would have gone with him."

"Aren't you free now?" asked Maria.

"Oh, my adopted father treats me like a small child. He thinks I'll always be satisfied looking after his goats. Well, I don't like just taking the goats to graze every day. I'm not a girl like you, I want to earn some money."

"You fool! Don't you know girls can earn money too? My sister works in Nairobi and she earns a lot of money."

"But girls are so weak," said Higiro.

Maria laughed. "Where are your parents?" she asked after a while.

"They are both dead."

"I'm sorry," she said. "Where's your home then?"

"I haven't really got one," he replied.

"Poor boy," Maria said sadly. "So you wanted to go to Kilembe with Kato?"

"How old is your brother?" Higiro asked.

"He's nearly seventeen, but he's big and strong and looks at least twenty. It's easy for such people to get jobs. But you, you look such a weakling and so young. I don't think many people would want to employ you."

"But I won't always remain like that. Boys grow into men and I'll become fat and strong like your brother."

"That will take about another four years," she said. "What will you do till then?"

"Look after goats with you," he replied, laughing and looking her full in the face.

"Don't be naughty," she began, and then she could not see the goats.

They both ran round to look for them, thinking they had gone into people's gardens. Then Maria remembered a place where they hid sometimes, and told Higiro to follow her.

"There they are!" she exclaimed with relief. After a few minutes, they looked through the trees and saw the goats had moved on to a greener pasture in another clearing. They were grazing peacefully.

Many hours passed and the sun became hotter and hotter. No animals moved around, the birds stopped their singing. Higiro and Maria sat under a tree and she opened her bag of food.

"Let's eat your food today and have mine tomorrow," Higiro said.

"No," she said in angry voice. "You eat your food and I'll eat mine."

"But I'm not used to eating alone," said Higiro.

"Then it's time you got used to it," she said and they started arguing.

"Let's share our food today and I'll ask my master

to give me something special tomorrow," said Higiro, not wanting to continue the quarrel.

Maria smiled. "All right," she agreed. "But if you don't bring something extra good tomorrow, I won't let you have any of my food again!"

They shared the food and Maria started eating without saying a prayer first.

"Maria, do you eat without saying the prayer to ask God to bless our food?" asked Higiro in a shocked voice.

"What do you mean by prayer?" Maria asked. "There's no such thing here in the forest."

Higiro smiled. "There's praying everywhere," he said. "Because God is everywhere. I'll teach you to pray."

"Pray to yourself, Higiro, but leave me alone."

The boy said a prayer quietly to himself before starting to eat.

"Who taught you how to pray?" asked Maria.

"My master and father," Higiro replied.

Maria concentrated on eating and said no more.

When Higiro had finished his food he fell asleep and Maria watched the goats. Late in the afternoon she woke him up and they rounded up the goats together and led them home.

"You had a good sleep today, didn't you?" Maria said as they were walking along.

"Yes, I did," replied Higiro. "I'm sorry you had to look after all the goats by yourself. You should have woken me up."

"I'll tell your master you go into the forest to sleep," Maria threatened him.

"Oh, please don't tell him that! Do you want him to be very angry with me?" Higiro cried.

"Well, promise that another time you won't sleep." She smiled at him.

"I promise I won't sleep!" said Higiro. "But you won't tell my master, will you?"

"I won't tell him," the girl replied.

"Thank you for your kindness to me. I like you for that," said Higiro.

When they were near their homes, the goats divided themselves into two groups and were willingly led back.

"Goodbye, and don't forget your promise," called Maria as she went.

"Goodbye," called Higiro. "I'll remember the food."

Higiro's master asked him many questions about his day in the forest, but Higiro said little, partly because he had already decided that he did not want to live that sort of life, and also because he did not want to upset his master.

After a good night's sleep, he awoke, refreshed, very early in the morning. His master who was already up told him to say his prayers and then clean out the goats' house before taking them into the forest. Higiro hated the horrible smell of the goats' house, but he cleaned it out and just as he had finished, he saw Maria come running along beside her goats. That reminded Higiro about the extra food.

"I must take some food today," he said to his master. "If I don't take enough, Maria won't let me eat with her. She gave me some of her food yesterday, and she said I must bring some for her today."

"Oh that girl!" said his master smiling. "All right, you'll have some extra food today."

So Higiro called to Maria and went back to the house for his food. Then he drove the goats out to meet her and they went into the forest.

The days passed, the weeks passed, the years passed, and Higiro's work was still to go into the forest with the goats. He was bored and felt that his life had come to a standstill. It was time he tried to find work in Kilembe mines. He was big enough now, he thought, and he wanted to be paid for his work. Why should he work for nothing?

"It's time I woke up and opened my eyes," he said to himself. "That's what my grandmother used to tell me."

The real problem facing Higiro was that he did not know where the mines were. He asked Maria but she did not know either, so his plan to run away to the mines was full of darkness. He did not know how to find out where he should go, so he had to follow his usual routine, taking the goats into the forest day after day.

"Let's sit down, I've something to tell you, Maria," said Higiro one day, after they had been wandering around for some time.

They sat down facing the herds of goats.

"You see, Maria," Higiro began, and then just looked at the girl and did not say anything else.

"I don't see anything," said Maria rather crossly. "Don't you know what you want to say?"

Silence followed as Higiro went on looking at Maria, feeling more and more shy.

"Why do you keep looking at me, smile and say nothing?" asked Maria.

"I think you know what I want to tell you," said Higiro.

"No, I don't," answered Maria. "If you don't tell me, how should I know?"

"Maria, Maria, my friend Maria, I love you!" he said at last.

Her reply surprised him. "Don't say that to me, you naughty boy. I don't want to hear those kind of words," she said in a serious voice.

"Why, you must love me, Maria?" he asked, looking hurt and upset.

"Why should I?" she asked in reply.

"Why not?" said Higiro, not knowing what else to say.

"It's too late!" she replied.

"Too late for what?" he asked.

"Too late to fall in love with me," she said.

"How can that be when you're so young?" asked Higiro.

"Because I am promised to somebody else," she said. "And you're too young and too poor to bother me!"

"There's no need to mention wealth. Everyone has to work hard to earn money and I'm not as young as you seem to think, Maria—please don't turn your face away from me! Listen to me, please listen! I'm old enough to be your husband."

Maria was completely confused at Higiro's words. She continued gazing into the distance, but said, "Go on talking. I can listen without looking at you."

Higiro continued. "Well, you see I've thought of a plan. I can go to the mines and work with your brother. I'll earn enough money to buy you all you need. I'll build you a big house."

"And what else?" asked Maria, smiling.

"We'll have goats and cows and grow our own food. I'll really make you very happy," said Higiro.

Maria shook her head. "Don't waste your words," she said firmly. "I told you that it's too late."

"Who have you promised to marry?" Higiro asked angrily.

"My brother who works in the mines," she replied.

"Oh God! Whoever would marry his sister?" exclaimed the horrified Higiro.

"You may call upon your God," Maria replied. "But Kato's mother is different from mine and so we can marry. Anyway it's none of your business whom I love and whom I marry."

"Maria, my good friend, I did not mean to annoy you and I'm sorry. I thought my words would please you," Higiro said.

"Well, at another time maybe they would have done," replied Maria.

"But it seems you are tempted too much and we know nothing about each other. Are your parents still alive?"

"No they died long ago, as I told you before. And yours?"

"Mine died long ago too," she said.

"But that man in the house where you live, isn't he your father?" asked Higiro.

"He's my uncle," she replied.

Silence again followed this remark. Then after a while Higiro asked Maria if she could remember anything her brother had said to give him some idea how he could find the mines.

"I'll tell you if you promise not to say anything about me to my brother. I don't want you even to tell him that you know me."

"Very well, I won't mention you at all. But tell me all you know," Higiro promised.

"I've never been there myself," Maria said. "But my brother is coming to see us tomorrow, so I'll ask him then."

"Can't I meet him?" asked Higiro eagerly. "I could ask him all I wanted to know about the mines."

"Very well, I'll introduce you, but don't say we go into the forest together every day."

The following day was a Saturday and when Kato arrived there was no one to greet him. However, he knew that Maria would be in the forest looking after the goats, because that was how he had started his working life. He had brought presents for his family, but he left these in the house and went out to find his sister.

Maria and Higiro were looking for fruits to eat when they heard a herdsman's whistle. It was the sound that people made when they were lost or calling for a friend in unknown places.

"Did you hear that sound?" asked Maria.

"Yes, who could it be?" asked Higiro, and then he gave an answering whistle.

Before long, a smart young man in a black suit came towards them. Was it a ghost? It could not be Kato. The last time Maria had seen him was before he had gone to Kilembe, dressed in old, torn, dirty rags. But yes, it was Kato! As he came nearer, Maria recognized his face. She ran towards him in great excitement.

"Oh Kato, why did you frighten us?" she said breathing heavily. "We thought you were a ghost!"

Then she introduced Higiro and they shook hands in a warm way.

"So you are looking after goats with my sister?" said Kato at once.

"Now tell us about the mines," begged Maria quietly. "What is it really like there?"

"It's an interesting place to be," replied Kato. "You meet people from many tribes, and all kinds of characters, drunkards, religious people, good, bad, married, unmarried, men and women."

"And young boys, too?" asked Higiro happily.

"Be quiet, Higiro. Let Kato finish telling us."

"We work very hard from sunrise to sunset," went on Kato. "We work for six days a week, but Sundays we are free. If you want to go off on Saturday you can but then you aren't paid for that day."

"Go on, tell us more!" said Maria.

"We're paid at the end of the month and on pay-days you see groups of people young and old, men and women, going happily to the 'Uhuru Bar'. Some go to the cinema and some buy clothes and other things from the shops. There are many shops near Kilembe, but things cost a lot of money."

"Where do you live?" asked Maria.

"Two workers share a room, but we have to pay for accommodation," he replied.

Higiro was listening to everything Kato said, but he was not really interested up to now. He wanted to talk to Kato about how he could set about finding a job at the mines. He waited until the next break in the conversation, then he asked, "Are there any jobs going now?"

"I can't really tell you," replied Kato. "If you're lucky, you could get one, I think."

"I'd like to come and work with you," said Higiro.

"That would be good, but will your master let you go to the mines? Who will look after the goats?" asked Kato.

"I'll escape," said Higiro excitedly.

"How will you do that?" asked Kato.

"I'll creep out during the night and go with you," replied Higiro.

"But I'm not leaving here at night. The bus to Kilembe goes at daybreak," answered Kato.

"That's all right," replied Higiro. "When you reach

the bus stop in the morning, I'll be there waiting for you."

"My friend, do you want to get me into trouble?" asked Kato. "Your master will be very angry with me. He'll think I came here to take you away. Anyhow, why do you want to go to the mines? You're very young and you don't look as if you could do the heavy work. If you leave here, who'll help my sister to look after the goats?"

"But I want to earn some money," replied Higiro. "My master hardly gives me anything, just a few old, torn clothes. They're too big for me as well, because they're the ones he has been wearing. I want to be able to buy new clothes and shoes, and I want to save enough money to build a house of my own."

"Listen my friend, I'll do my best to help you, but not just now," said Kato. "We've got to make your master understand that it was nothing to do with me that you ran away. I'll go back to Kilembe tomorrow, but you must not come with me. I'll find another type of job for you and you can try for work at the mines later. Tomorrow afternoon, I'll go to the small town, Kisuli. That's where you must meet me. Go into the forest with Maria as usual, but leave her looking after the goats alone."

Kato then turned to Maria. "When you drive the goats back home that evening, you must pretend that Higiro went off chasing some goats that had strayed and that he never came back."

"But what will his uncle think happened to him?" asked Maria.

"He'll think he was swallowed by one of the large snakes that eat goats and calves. Then he'll go and report his absence to the village chief."

"What will happen after that?" asked Higiro.

"The chief will order the men in the village to search for you in the forest. They won't find you and they won't find the snake and they will all think you're dead and that will be the end. But when I get you a job, Higiro, you must pay me for all the trouble I have taken," said Kato. "Now, you must agree to this before I do anything at all for you."

Higiro knelt before the well-dressed Kato. "I will, Sir," he said.

But Maria complained. "Brother, I think yours is a very bad plan. It's too much work for me to look after all the goats by myself. Take me with you. I'm not going to stay here alone."

"Sister, remember our promise. It's not yet time. You must be patient and wait a while longer," said Kato.

"Then leave me some money to buy necklaces and bracelets," she pleaded.

"I've brought you enough money to buy the pretty things you want," said Kato. "But now I must go to Kisuli where I'll spend the night, and then tomorrow I'll go back to Kilembe."

"Why can't you spend the night at our uncle's house?" asked his sister.

"No, that's too humble a place for me now," said Kato in a superior voice. "I'm used to better rooms and a soft bed."

"You can say that now, but you never minded where you slept when we used to go into the forest together," said Maria.

"No, I didn't think of such things then," replied Kato. "But you'll feel the same in future when you keep your part of our promise."

There was silence for a few moments.

"Here's a hundred shillings," said Kato. "Buy anything you want for yourself with that, and here's fifty shillings to give to uncle to buy sugar and salt."

Maria took the money and thanked him happily.

"When are you coming to see us again?" she asked.

"Don't worry. It won't be long, you'll just see me come!" he replied laughing. Maria laughed too.

"Goodbye for now, Higiro," said Kato. "Don't forget, on Sunday afternoon I shall be waiting for you at Kisuli."

"Where are the goats, Maria?" Higiro asked when Kato had gone.

"I've no idea where they've gone," said Maria. "I'd forgotten all about them."

"We'd better look for them," said Higiro. "I hope they haven't gone into the people's gardens."

They both ran here and there looking for the goats, and at last they found them feeding quietly in a grassy clearing. At dusk they led them home, and so another day ended.

That night Higiro dreamt he was working in the mines, and when he awoke, he prayed that his dreams would come true.

Chapter 6

The Escape

Higiro woke up very early on Sunday morning with the idea of a fresh opportunity burning in his mind. The great day had come. The day to start his journey to the mines.

His master knew nothing of his plan, but was surprised when he saw Higiro was awake so early.

"Couldn't you sleep?" he asked. "Not very well," Higiro replied. "There were so many mosquitoes buzzing around."

"I'm sorry they kept you awake. Here's your food and Maria is just coming. I hope you have a peaceful day in the forest," Higiro's master said, and went about his business. Higiro greeted Maria and drove out the goats as usual.

"You're going to the mines today," she said. "Please greet my brother for me."

"I'll greet him from both of us," he said. "Oh its raining now. Perhaps that will stop you from going," said Maria.

"Nothing will stop me from going to Kisuli," replied Higiro confidently.

"Do you really think that my brother will come to Kisuli for you?" asked Maria.

"Yes, I am sure he will," replied Higiro.

"You can't really tell," said Maria to herself, as she remembered how Kato used to play tricks on people and enjoy the fun when he succeeded.

They walked on into the forest and when they had gone a long way, they decided to sit down and rest.

"You're going to leave me alone soon, aren't you?" asked Maria.

"Not just yet, it's too early to go now," replied Higiro.

"You'll remember me when you're working in the mines, won't you?" Maria asked.

"How can I even try to think of you when you refused me?" said Higiro.

"I didn't refuse you," she said, "anyway, I'm asking you to remember me as a friend who spent the days in the forest with you, not as your future wife."

"I shall remember you," said Higiro looking at her. "But will you promise to marry me?"

"Don't assume so much," was her reply.

It started raining heavily as they went on talking, so they ran to take shelter under a big tree. But the rain poured through the branches, and Higiro's dirty old clothes became wetter and wetter and he started shivering with cold. Maria was luckier as she always carried a piece of cloth with which to cover her head and body when it rained. When she saw Higiro shivering with cold, she called him to share the protection of her cloth. Higiro was annoyed that she had waited until he was soaking wet before she asked him. However, he went over and sat near her body beside him, as she covered him with her piece of cloth.

The rain went on and on until after the time that Higiro should have started for Kisuli.

"I must go now," he said as soon as the rain stopped.

"It's not time yet," said Maria.

"You know I must reach the place before your brother gets there," said Higiro. "Now don't forget to tell my master exactly what your brother told you to say the other day."

But Maria tried to stop Higiro from leaving her.

She felt lonely as a child who sees his parents going off to work every morning.

"Higiro," she called. "We've been together in the forest every day for a long, long time, and now you're leaving me. Give me something that will remind me of you."

"I've nothing to give you," Higiro told her.

"Give me some money," begged Maria. "Then I can buy something to remind me of you."

"You know I've no money," replied Higiro.

"Leave me your old stick then."

"You can have that, I'll not need it any more. Here you are," said Higiro, holding out the stick. "Keep it with you always. Now I must go. Goodbye, God be with you."

"Before you go..." Maria said softly.

Higiro turned round. He could not understand what Maria wanted, and he was impatient to be off as all he could think about was his journey. Maria walked towards him and threw her arms round his neck. She pulled him towards her and kissed him.

"Oh Higiro, I do love you," she said. "Do you love me?"

"I love you," he replied, still anxious to be off.

"Then promise you'll come back to see me as soon as you can."

"I'll do that," he answered quickly. But it was the wrong time for Maria to talk about love. Higiro made it quite clear he wanted to go. He could not think of love at that moment, but only of his journey to the mines and his future work. He pulled himself away from her and ran in the direction of Kisuli without looking back.

Higiro arrived earlier than he expected, so he found a hotel and sat down on the verandah to wait for Kato. He enjoyed watching the people and the traffic. He could see the bus stop from where he was sitting, and as everyone got out of the buses he looked to see if his friend Kato was amongst them. He waited until the last bus of the day arrived from Kilembe. "Kato must be on this one," he said to himself, and ran to greet him. One by one, he watched the passengers get out, but Kato was not there. The last person to get down was the driver, and then the bus was empty.

What had happened? Had Kato deceived him? Surely Not! Kato was a gentleman. Then Higiro remembered that Maria had asked him if her brother had definitely agreed to meet him. Higiro had believed he would come, but Kato had not actually promised. The truth was that Higiro had been deceived.

He went back to the hotel verandah and waited and waited, but Kato did not come. Darkness fell and Higiro wondered how to find his way back home. No, that would be no good. By now Maria would have told his master that he was lost in the forest. If he went back his master would beat him.

"I shan't go back," Higiro said to himself. "If Kato doesn't come, I'll find the way to Kilembe by myself."

He waited another few hours and when Kato did not appear, he knew he had been fooled. He got up and walked up and down the streets of Kisuli. There were lots of people around and he wanted to talk to them, but he was a stranger and dared not approach them. At last he saw an old man who looked as if he had a kind face. Higiro stopped and greeted him. Then he asked for the way to Kilembe.

"You must first take a bus to Kampala," said the old man. "And from there you will find another bus that goes to Kilembe. But there aren't any more buses tonight, you'll have to start your journey in the morning."

Higiro thanked him, and walked on. Where could he stay for the night? Would some kind person give him a bed? He knew how dirty he was. Who would welcome a boy dressed in rags who looked like a thief? He decided no one would take the risk of having him in their house, so when he came to the main road, he started walking along the direction of Kampala. He walked and walked, recalling his early days when he had walked from Rwanda with his father.

"I must be brave like my father was," he told himself. "I'll walk all night without asking anybody to give me a bed."

It was lonely on the road and only few cars passed him. No one was walking at that late hour. He went on and on until at last he heard the birds start their morning song and the day began to dawn. It was only then that he felt he must stop and rest. He found a place off the road under a tree where he lay down and soon fell asleep.

When Higiro awoke, the sun was high in the sky and he saw many cars speeding along the road. He had a little money with him, so he decided to stop the first car he could. He thought all cars were taxis, so he stood in the middle of the road and put out his hand. A car stopped and the driver got out and spoke in an angry voice. Higiro did not understand what he said, so he showed him his money and said Kampala. The man looked at the dirty boy and shook his head.

Higiro was very disappointed but he moved to the side of the road and the man got back in his car and drove away.

In a few moments a taxi came along at great speed. Higiro stepped into the middle of the road again and waved his arms. The driver screeched to a halt and got out. He was furious with Higiro and hit him on both cheeks and pushed him to the side of the road. Higiro tried to tell him that he wanted to get to Kampala, but he was too upset to speak and instead he started crying. The driver saw that the boy had

some money in his hand and he thought he might be another paying passenger, which he needed.

"What do you want?" he asked roughly.

"I've got to go to Kampala, can you take me?" asked Higiro.

"Have you two shillings?" asked the man.

"Yes—here!" Higiro said quickly and handed him the money.

"Get in quickly then," said the driver. "Sit behind the others. Oh, his clothes do smell, poor boy," he murmured to himself. "Now boy," he went on before he started off again. "You don't stop cars by standing in the middle of the road. If you do that, you might easily be knocked down, and people will think you're mad anyway. Next time, stand at the side of the road and wave your arm up and down."

"Yes, sir, thank you sir," said Higiro. He felt happy once the car started. He would soon be in Kampala and then he would find a car or a bus going to Kilembe.

"Where are you going boy?" asked the driver.

"To Kampala," replied Higiro.

"Yes, I know. But which part of Kampala?"

"Kilembe," said Higiro confidently. *I am a fool,*

Kilembe isn't in Kampala, he thought immediately he had spoken.

Everybody in the car laughed and looked round at Higiro. He was now the centre of interest and he felt happy and laughed too.

"You've a friend in Kilembe, boy?" asked the driver.

"Yes, Kato's my friend. He's working there and I'm going to work with him."

"I don't know who this Kato is but if you give me more money I'll take you to the bus station."

"How much sir?"

"Four more shillings," said the driver.

Higiro handed him a five-shilling note, and the driver did give him a shilling change when he stopped to pick up more passengers. Wherever he stopped, he said to Higiro, "Did you see how this man stopped the car?"

And Higiro replied, "Yes now I've learnt. Now I understand."

At last they came to the city. Higiro had never been there before and he found it very strange to see so many people. Then he realised how clean they all looked and he knew he looked untidy and dirty. As the taxi driver slowly passed the shops, he wondered if he could find a job in one of them but no, he was going to Kilembe and he must not change his mind.

The taxi stopped at the car park and Higiro saw boys washing the cars and men repairing them, all looking as dirty as himself. Perhaps that was the sort of job he should get. But no, he told himself firmly, he must go on to Kilembe. Most people got out of the taxi and Higiro could hear other taxi drivers shouting, "Jinja, Masaka," and many people hurried towards them.

The driver took Higiro to the bus station and showed him which bus was going to Kilembe. Higiro thanked him and climbed up the steps but before he had time to sit down, the conductor went up to him and asked for the fare.

"How much is it, sir?" Higiro asked.

"Where are you going?"

"To Kilembe."

"How old are you?"

"Twen-ten years, sir."

"Stop shivering. What's the matter with you?" asked the bus conductor crossly. "Give me twelve shillings."

Higiro handed him his twenty-shilling note and the conductor gave him a ticket.

"I haven't any change just now," he said. "Remind me to give it to you before you get out."

Higiro nodded his head as he had seen older people do, and sat down.

The bus soon started off and travelled the whole day long. Higiro felt hungry and thirsty, as he had not brought anything to eat or drink. There was no chance of buying anything as the bus did not stop. At last Higiro fell asleep until he heard the bus driver telling the passengers that they had reached their journey's end. They had arrived at Kilembe. The passengers all got out and Higiro quite forgot to ask the conductor for his eight shillings change. The conductor remembered but did not say anything.

Higiro jumped off the bus and walked up and down the streets, hoping to see Kato. After a time, he felt hungry again and decided to buy something to eat. He felt in his pockets and found only one shilling. Then he remembered his change and ran back to the bus station and found the bus which had brought him to Kilembe.

"Please, sir, my money, my change—I forgot to ask you for it, but you said you'd give it to me at Kilembe, and we're at Kilembe now."

"Show me your ticket," said the bus conductor. Higiro felt in both pockets, but he could not find his ticket.

"I'm afraid I've lost it," he replied.

"Then I can't give you the money," said the conductor.

"But it's eight shillings, I must have it," said the boy, and he started to cry.

People crowded round and there was a lot of argument, but no one could help the boy. He had lost his ticket and the conductor refused to give him the money.

Higiro walked sadly away along the streets looking for Kato.

"Where was Kato? Why hadn't he come? Was he still working in the mines? Where were the mines and how could he get there?"

These questions kept burning in Higiro's mind. Darkness was near and he wondered where he could spend the night. He walked into one of the shops and asked if anybody there knew a man called Kato. Nobody seemed to know and only one man understood Higiro's language.

"Where do you come from?" he asked the boy.

Higiro explained why he was in Kilembe and as the man seemed to be sympathetic towards him, he asked if he could stay the night. He was lucky! The man was kind and gave him an old mattress and blanket and told him to sleep in a room leading off the kitchen. The warmth from the kitchen fire made the room warm and it smelt good. Higiro felt at peace and slept soundly all through the night.

Chapter 7

Will Higiro Meet Kato?

The following morning Higiro was woken up by the owner of the house and given some work to do. He was told to wash the car and the lorry and sweep round the compound of the shop. Higiro was not paid much for these duties, but he did not mind because he had been told he would be given more money if he worked well. Higiro did the same jobs every day but sometimes he had more interesting work as well.

One day he was told to go to Kampala with the lorry driver and help him buy supplies for the shop. Higiro was glad to be going to Kampala again, and ran to ask the lorry driver how he could help him.

"Go to the store behind the shop and fetch twenty empty sacks and throw them in the back of the lorry," said the driver. "Then fill a tin with water in case we want a drink on the way."

When Higiro had done this, he climbed into the front seat of the lorry and the driver started the engine. There was silence for some time and Higiro

started day dreaming. He was leading a new life as the driver's assistant.

"What part of the world do you come from?" asked the driver, when they had travelled some miles.

Higiro thought for a time, then he answered, "From many parts."

"Tell me their names," said the man.

"Well, I was born in Rwanda," began Higiro. "I can't remember the other places, but misfortune brought me this way."

Silence followed and Higiro felt uncomfortable. He

did not want to be asked where he came from.

"Are your parents alive?" enquired the lorry driver.

"They died long ago," replied Higiro softly.

"That's rotten luck, boy. But you shouldn't worry too much. Lots of people have lost their parents."

"Are your parents dead, too?" asked Higiro.

"They died a long time ago, and I'm quite used to living without them," said the driver. "Don't you have any relatives living nearby?"

"I've nobody I know in this area and no friend to talk to except my God," Higiro replied. "He gives me great comfort," he added seriously.

How old are you boy?"

"I'm not sure," replied Higiro thinking hard. "Fourteen, I think, or perhaps fifteen."

"You certainly don't look more than that," said the driver. "You're still a child really. Haven't you any relatives anywhere?"

"No, none at all," the boy replied.

"Have you ever been to school?"

"Yes, in Rwanda, but only for three months," Higiro said.

"That wasn't long enough to give you any real knowledge," remarked the lorry driver. Then he drove to a petrol station and asked the attendant for twenty-five shillings worth of petrol. "And hurry up, please, I've no time to waste."

At that moment another lorry drew up and the driver asked for petrol as well. The attendant was confused and started to serve the second man first. The lorry driver with Higiro was furious and shouted, "What are you doing? Why are you serving the man who came after me? Don't you know your job?"

The attendant became frightened and looked up and down and ran here and there touching one thing and another, but not doing anything helpful. The lorry driver started shouting at him again and then the petrol attendant went and served him.

"These petrol attendants are so stupid sometimes," said the lorry driver as he started off again. Higiro did not make any comment but asked how far it was to Kampala.

"We're nearly there," replied the driver still annoyed.

"Are you going back as soon as we've bought the things, or shall we spend the night at Kato's place?" asked Higiro.

"What's your name?" asked the man, not replying to the question.

"Higiro, sir," the boy replied.

"You're not Higiro sir, you're Higiro," the driver joked.

The boy laughed and the lorry driver forgot his anger, but a new idea was forming in his mind.

"Higiro, I'm going to talk to you like a father," he said seriously.

Higiro sat up ready to listen to what the man had to say.

"When we reach Kampala, we'll go and see Mr. Kato. My idea is for you to join him in business now. I'll lend you the necessary money, and I hope you'll pay me back when you're better off," said the lorry driver.

"Oh thank you, thank you!" cried Higiro happily,

hardly able to believe his good fortune.

"Don't thank me yet," said the driver. "But make sure you don't turn out like some other young men. I mean don't forget the person who helped you when you were poor. I'll talk to Kato about all this."

"You're very good to me, sir. But what shall I do about my new master at Kilembe?" asked Higiro.

"Don't worry about him. When I go back I'll tell him you disappeared when I was in the city and I couldn't find you."

"How much money are you going to lend me, sir?"

"I'll discuss with Kato and then I'll tell you," replied the man.

"Do you think Kato will agree to have me?" asked Higiro.

"Oh yes, I'm sure he will. Last time I was there he said he wanted an assistant in his shop. Let's hope he likes you."

"When do I have to pay you back?" asked Higiro in a worried voice.

"I'll tell you when it's time—it won't be until you're

making money," said the driver.

Higiro could still hardly believe his good fortune. To be given money without even having to struggle for it! Was this really a dream? Or had he come to a place where people threw money away? He was confused with all these thoughts, but he had forgotten one important matter. The driver was not going to give the money to him. He had said he would give it to Kato.

Still the profits were to be his, and anyway, it depended on whether or not Kato agreed to the plan.

The lorry stopped at Kato's shop and Kato came out to welcome his friend, the driver. He was surprised when he saw Higiro and rather hoped it was someone else with a similar face. No, it was Higiro, he realised when he went near him.

"How's business? Why is the shop empty? Where are the customers?" asked the driver.

"Business is not good," replied Kato. "It's a bad time of the year for shopkeepers. Many of them are having a sale to attract customers and so no one seems to come to this shop."

"What do you do all day?" asked the driver. "Just

sit around?"

"More or less," moaned Kato. "Some days I sell five or ten shillings' worth of goods. That's about all."

"That's bad, boy. But don't worry, your time will come."

"How are things with you?" Kato asked the driver, looking at Higiro meanwhile.

"Not bad. Not bad at all," he replied. "Now tell me, do you know this boy?" he asked, pushing Higiro forward.

"Yes, yes. He's my old friend Higiro. How did you meet him?" asked Kato.

"Never mind about that. I've brought him here to help you in the shop. I'm going to give you some money to buy more goods to fill your shop. Then you must learn how to arrange everything and make your shop look better than others. That's the way to attract more customers. If your shop is dirty and untidy, people with a lot of money to spend certainly won't come. They'll go somewhere else."

"Yes, I agree with your advice," said Kato. "Someone from the Ministry of Labour was talking on the radio last night, and he said much the same thing. You leave Higiro to help me and I'll try to do better in future."

"Very well. You do that. Here's the money. I must go now. Goodbye Kato! Goodbye Higiro! I'll be coming to see you soon."

Kato and Higiro waved goodbye and they were left alone together. They looked at each other, both with questions in their mind.

"Welcome to Kampala," said Kato at last. "But tell me, how did you come to know this man?"

Higiro did not reply.

"Talk, boy talk. What's the matter with you?"

Higiro took a deep breath and started, "I nearly died on the way looking for you."

"Well, forget that, my friend. You've found me now," replied Kato, deciding not to question him any more.

"When did you come here?" asked Higiro.

"Not so long ago," replied Kato.

"Do you make a lot of money in the shop?"

"Not very much. I'm still new here and not many people know me yet."

"We'll soon make money, I'm sure."

"How?"

"You'll see."

"Would you like a drink?" asked Kato. "I've two bottles of beer."

"I'd like a drink, but I don't want beer. I'll have some water," replied Higiro.

"Tell me, how much do you know about this lorry driver?" asked Kato when he had given Higiro a mug of water.

"He seems to be a clever man. He's a friend of mine."

"How clever?"

"Well, he makes a lot of money by lending it to people and then they give him double the amount when they pay him back. In that way, he's becoming very rich."

"What happens if anyone doesn't pay him?" asked Kato.

"He just comes to your house or shop and sells your property until he has the amount you owe him."

"Well, he is a clever man," said Kato.

"I hope we can pay him back by the end of next month. But we must work hard to earn enough to pay him or he'll be very annoyed."

"Yes, we must work hard. Business people are hard-working, so we'll manage to pay him somehow."

Evening came and they knew they would have no more customers that day, so they closed the shop, had a meal and went to bed.

Higiro felt happy. Here he was, working with Kato, whom he never expected to see again. He resolved to start afresh and work very hard so he would be able to stand up to town life.

Chapter 8

Town Life

The shop was in Wandegeya, a suburb of Kampala. Life there was very different for Higiro. There were films and bars and football stadiums and many other places of entertainment. Kato took Higiro out and he especially liked going to bars. His favourite bar was called "City Bar" and the first time they went was on a Saturday evening. It was full of people and Milly Small's records were playing on the jukebox. Everybody was excited and happy; fat and busy barmaids were serving the drinks.

They sat down and a barmaid came running up to them. She smiled at Kato as if they were already friends.

"What will you have today?" she asked.

"A bottle of warm Bell, please," said Kato.

"And what about your friend?"

Kato looked at Higiro and Higiro looked at Kato. Higiro had no idea what to order, so Kato said, "Bring him a cold Tiger please!"

The fat barmaid rolled back to the bar and ordered the beer, which she quickly brought to the table.

At first Higiro thought the Tiger tasted very bitter, but he kept on sipping it until he got used to it. The juke-box went on playing and more people flocked in. The noise became deafening, people started dancing, and the whole place started smelling of beer, sweat and cigarette smoke. Higiro was beginning to warm up. He finished his first Tiger and ordered another, but he knew they were wasting money when they should be saving it.

"Friend Kato, we're wasting so much money in this bar. Let's leave and go home."

"Yes friend, I know, but what's money for anyway?" asked Kato with the voice of a drunken man. "Anyway, we're not wasting money. We're spending it!"

"It's not good spending," said Higiro.

"Remember money eaten is your own money."

"So?"

"So let's drink and drink until our bellies can take no more."

"Have you forgotten the man who lent me the money? I've got to pay him back," Higiro reminded him.

"Yes, we'll pay him."

"But when?"

"I'll tell you, when we're at home. Now drink up and forget all about that."

"Yes sir," replied Higiro weakly.

However, in spite of Kato's drinking, they managed to pay back the borrowed money at the end of the month. But the visits to the bar and the drinking went on, week after week, month after month, and at the end of the year the two traders found that instead of making a profit, they were in debt.

Higiro had said before that drinking would ruin their business, and his friend, the lorry-driver had told him how bad drink was. Now the truth of his friend's wisdom was clear.

"What shall we do now?" asked Higiro. "We've failed to make a profit."

"Well, there's only one thing to do and that's to pay all our debts from our own money, or the shop will be closed by our creditors."

"But I've no money of my own," said Higiro.

"Neither have I," said Kato.

"How much do we owe our creditors?"

"Seven hundred shillings, and if we don't pay them at the end of the month, all the people who sold goods to us will come and take them away."

"Then we must sell all the things cheaply so lots of people will come and buy them. At least we'll get some money that way," suggested Higiro.

They had a grand sale in the shop and when everything had gone, they were able to pay their debts and there was some money left over. But Higiro was annoyed. His friend had fooled him. He was also poor, thoughtless and a drunkard.

One day after work, Higiro told Kato he wanted to leave.

"To go where?" asked Kato.

"Anywhere."

"So?"

"So I want you to give me my part of the money."

"You want to leave me alone, don't you?"

"It's not just that."

'You know I haven't got much money at the moment."

"Give me anything you can, as long as it's more than three hundred shillings," said Higiro.

"I won't stop you going, I'll call a friend to witness my giving you the money."

"Can't we just agree between ourselves?"

"All right, but wait until tomorrow," said Kato.

Morning came and Higiro packed his things and when he was ready to go, Kato gave him exactly three hundred shillings.

"Who are you going to work with now?" he asked.

"I'm going to marry your sister and we'll work together."

Now Kato was really angry. Who had put such an idea into his head? His sister marrying Higiro? He must be mad!

"You won't marry my sister! Anyway you're too poor to pay the dowry," shouted Kato.

"I'll pay as I earn the money," said Higiro.

"Before you thought about that you should have asked me whether or not I would allow you to marry my sister. I say you will not marry her!"

"Why should I ask you?" said Higiro, remembering what Maria had said about promising to marry Kato, who was not really her brother at all.

They argued and argued, until Higiro left and travelled to Bwaise, another suburb of Kampala. He started a shop of his own and this time he was very successful.

After some years, he married a girl called Maria. The name pleased him because it reminded him of his first love, whom he never met again.

www.ingramcontent.com/pod-product-compliance
Lightning Source LLC
Chambersburg PA
CBHW041210150726
48006CB00016B/2195